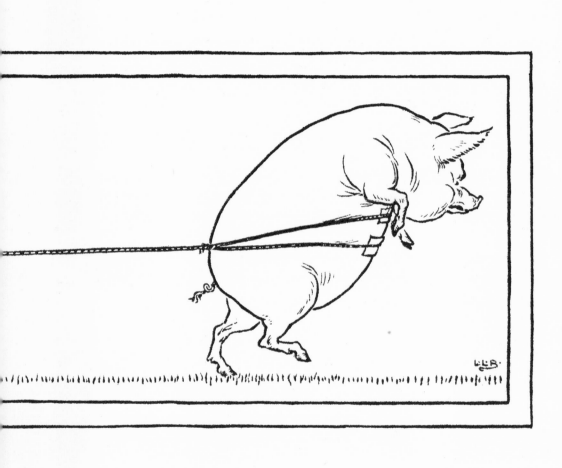

RING O' ROSES

RING O' ROSES

A NURSERY RHYME PICTURE BOOK

With numerous Drawings in
Colour and Black-and-White
by
L. LESLIE BROOKE

LONDON
FREDERICK WARNE & CO. LTD.
AND NEW YORK

THE MAN IN THE MOON

THE Man in the Moon
    Came tumbling down,
And asked his way to Norwich;

They told him south,
And he burnt his mouth
With eating cold pease-porridge.

TO MARKET, TO MARKET

TO market, to market, to buy a fat Pig;
Home again, home again, dancing a jig.

To market, to market, to buy a fat Hog;
Home again, home again, jiggety-jog.

THERE WAS A MAN

THERE was a man, and he had nought,
    And robbers came to rob him;

He crept up to the chimney-pot,

AND THEN THEY THOUGHT THEY HAD HIM

BUT HE GOT DOWN ON T'OTHER SIDE

And then they could not find him;

He ran fourteen miles in fifteen days,
And never looked behind him.

THE LION AND THE UNICORN

THE Lion and the Unicorn
    Were fighting for the crown;
The Lion beat the unicorn
    All round about the town.

Some gave them white bread,
   And some gave them brown;
Some gave them plum-cake,
   And sent them out of town.

LITTLE MISS
MUFFET

LITTLE Miss Muffet
Sat on a tuffet
Eating of curds and
whey;

There came a big Spider
And sat down beside her,
And frightened Miss Muffet away.

ORANGES AND LEMONS

ORANGES AND LEMONS

Gay go up, and gay go down
To ring the bells of London Town.

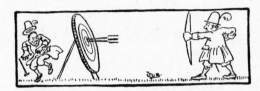

BULL'S eyes and targets,
Say the bells of St. Marg'ret's.

Brickbats and tiles,   Pancakes and fritters,
Say the bells of St. Giles'.   Say the bells of St. Peter's.

Two sticks and an apple,
Say the bells at Whitechapel.

Halfpence and farthings,
Say the bells of St. Martin's.

Oranges and Lemons,
Say the bells of St. Clement's.

Old Father Baldpate,
Say the slow bells at Aldgate.

Pokers and tongs,
Say the bells of St. John's.

Kettles and pans,
Say the bells of St. Ann's.

You owe me ten shillings,
Say the bells at St. Helen's.

When will you pay me?
Say the bells at Old Bailey.

When I grow rich,
Say the bells at Shoreditch.

Pray when will that be?
Say the bells of Stepney.

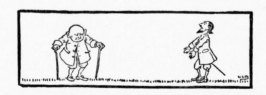

I am sure I don't know,
Says the great bell of Bow.

Here comes a candle to light you to bed,
And here comes a chopper to chop off your head.

GOOSEY, GOOSEY GANDER

GOOSEY, Goosey Gander,
  Where shall I wander?

Upstairs, downstairs,
And in my lady's chamber.

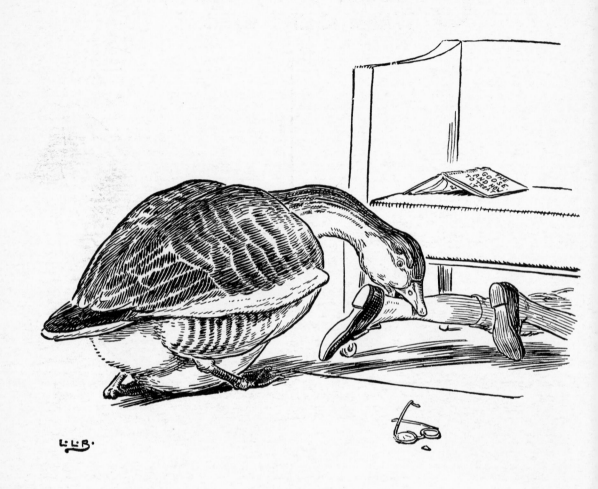

There I met an old man
　　That would not say his prayers:
I took him by the left leg,
　　And threw him downstairs.

HUMPTY DUMPTY

HUMPTY DUMPTY sat on a wall;

Humpty Dumpty had a great fall;

All the King's horses and all the King's men
Couldn't put Humpty Dumpty together again.

BAA, BAA, BLACK SHEEP

BAA, baa, Black Sheep,
    Have you any wool?
Yes, marry, have I,
    Three bags full:

One for my master,
    And one for my Dame,
And one for the little boy
    That lives in the lane!

THE THREE WISE MEN OF GOTHAM

THREE wise men of Gotham
Went to sea in a bowl:

If the bowl had been stronger,
  My song would have been longer.

THIS LITTLE PIG WENT
TO MARKET

THIS little pig went to market;

This little pig stayed at home;

This little pig had roast beef;
        This little pig had none;

This little pig cried "Wee, wee, wee!
I can't find my way

home !''

JACK AND JILL

JACK and Jill went up the hill
　　To fetch a pail of water;
Jack fell down and broke his crown,
　　And Jill came tumbling after.

SIMPLE SIMON

SIMPLE SIMON met a pieman,
Going to the fair;

Says Simple Simon to the pieman,
"Let me taste your ware."

Says the pieman to Simple Simon,
"Do you mean to pay?"
Says Simon, "Yes, of course I do!"
And then he ran away.

Simple Simon went a-fishing
For to catch a whale:
All the water he had got
Was in his mother's pail.

THERE WAS A CROOKED MAN

THERE was a crooked man, and he went
a crooked mile,
He found a crooked sixpence against a crooked
stile:

He bought a crooked cat, which caught a
   crooked mouse,
And they all lived together in a crooked
   little house.

LITTLE BO-PEEP

LITTLE BO-PEEP

LITTLE BO-PEEP has lost her sheep,
  And can't tell where to find them;
Leave them alone, and they'll come home,
  And bring their tails behind them.

Little Bo-peep fell fast asleep,
  And dreamt she heard them bleating;
But when she awoke, she found it a joke,
  For they were still a-fleeting.

Then up she took her little crook,
  Determined for to find them;
She found them indeed, but it made her
    heart bleed,
  For they'd left all their tails behind 'em.

RING O' ROSES

RING a ring o' roses,
  A pocket full of posies;
Hush! hush! hush!
  And we all tumble down.

THERE WAS A LITTLE MAN

THERE was a little man,
  And he had a little gun,
And his bullets were made of lead, lead, lead;
He went to the brook
And saw a little duck,
And he shot it right through the head, head, head.

He carried it home
To his old wife Joan,
And bid her a fire for to make, make, make;
To roast the little duck
He had shot in the brook,
And he'd go and fetch her the drake, drake, drake.

GOOD KING ARTHUR

WHEN good king Arthur ruled this land,
　　He was a goodly king;
He stole three pecks of barley-meal,
　　To make a bag-pudding.

A bag-pudding the king did make,
　　And stuffed it well with plums:
And in it put great lumps of fat,
　　As big as my two thumbs.

The king and queen did eat thereof,
    And noblemen beside;
And what they could not eat that night,
    The queen next morning fried.

To Market - 1 Mile

HICKETY PICKETY MY BLACK HEN

HICKETY, pickety, my black hen,
She lays eggs for gentlemen;

Gentlemen come every day
To see what my black hen doth lay.

COCK-A-DOODLE-DOO

COCK-a-doodle-doo!
My dame has lost her shoe;
My master's lost his fiddling-stick,
And don't know what to do.

Cock-a-doodle-doo!
What is my dame to do?
Till master finds his fiddling-stick,
She'll dance without her shoe.

Cock-a-doodle-doo!
My dame has lost her shoe,
And master's found his fiddling-stick;
Sing doodle-doodle-doo!

Cock-a-doodle-doo!
My dame will dance with you,
While master fiddles his fiddling-stick,
For dame and doodle-doo.

Cock-a-doodle-doo!
Dame has lost her shoe;
Gone to bed and scratched her head,
And can't tell what to do.

L·L·B·

WEE WILLIE WINKIE

WEE Willie Winkie runs through the town,
    Upstairs and downstairs in his nightgown,
Rapping at the window, crying through the lock,
"Are the children in their beds, for now it's eight
        o'clock?"